AMANDA'S PERFECT HAIR

by LINDA MILSTEIN

pictures by SUSAN MEDDAUGH

TAMBOURINE BOOKS   NEW YORK

For Noah and Zena, may they
always follow their hearts
L.M.

For Marguerite and Harry
S.M.

Text copyright © 1993 by Linda Breiner Milstein
Illustrations copyright © 1993 by Susan Meddaugh

Tambourine Books, a division of William Morrow & Company, Inc.,
1350 Avenue of the Americas, New York, New York 10019.
Printed in Hong Kong by South China Printing Company (1988) Ltd.

Library of Congress Cataloging in Publication Data

Milstein, Linda Breiner. Amanda's perfect hair/by Linda Breiner Milstein;
pictures by Susan Meddaugh. — 1st ed. p. cm.
Summary: Although everyone else keeps telling Amanda how wonderful
her long thick hair is, she decides that she doesn't like it.
[1. Hair — Fiction.] I. Meddaugh, Susan, ill. II. Title.
PZ7.M6446Am 1993 [E] — dc20 92-34314 CIP AC
ISBN 0-688-11153-X. — ISBN 0-688-11154-8 (lib. bdg.)
1 3 5 7 9 10 8 6 4 2
FIRST EDITION

When Amanda walked into a room,
her hair seemed to enter first.

Everyone would turn and look and murmur, "Oh, what pretty hair." Then they would notice Amanda.

Amanda didn't like that.

More than anything else in the whole wide world, Amanda wanted different hair.

Amanda's hair was longer than long and thicker than thick.
It took an hour to wash and rinse! It took two hours to
dry! Amanda didn't like that either.

It hurt when she sat on it.

It hurt when it got stuck in her jacket and it hurt when it got caught in the door.

Amanda didn't like *any* of that.

Amanda thought about her hair all the time. She tried to discuss it. Everybody had something to say about it, but nobody would listen.

"Your hair is so lovely," said her teacher. "You look like Alice in Wonderland." Her teacher was always talking about people in books.

Today is Wednesday.
We go to Library.
We meet with our
Reading Buddies.
Niko is line leader.

But Amanda did not want to look like Alice in Wonderland.
Alice already looked like that. Amanda wanted to look
like herself.

"Your hair is so pretty," said the next-door neighbor. "It's like Niagara Falls." The next-door neighbor had four sons and wished that she had a girl with long hair.

Amanda did not want to look like a waterfall. Amanda wanted to look like a girl.

Scenic AMANDA FALLS

"Your hair is so beautiful," said her mother. "People would give their eye teeth to have hair like you." Amanda's mother had fine straight hair that never ever curled.

What would she do with extra teeth? Wear them as a necklace? No, Amanda already had plenty of teeth and a nice necklace of her own, too.

It does have character, thought Amanda.

But then again, her big sister said, "Next Halloween you won't need a costume. When it's down you look like a witch."

Amanda had no intention of being a witch. Her big sister always said things like that. Amanda didn't listen to a word she said.

Her little brother said, "Keep it just the way it is. When you braid it at night, it looks like a python slithering down a tree."

But Amanda didn't want to be a jungle. Her brother always said weird things. She never listened to him either.

Her father said, "Your wavy hair is like a river going out to sea. You wouldn't be my girl without it."

He was joking, as usual. Amanda knew he would always be her father. Besides, it was hard enough just being Amanda sometimes, without being a river, too.

Her friends said they had so much fun inventing wonderful new hairdos for her.

But Amanda did not like being their experiment, even if they were her best friends.

But, maybe it really was the best thing about her. Maybe it was what made her special.

Then again, maybe not, thought Amanda.

"That's it!" she said, and went into the bathroom and closed the door.

"Come out!" "Don't do it!" "Open the door!"
"No, Amanda!" everybody yelled.

Snip. Snip. Snip.

"No! No! Not your long, thick, beautiful, curly, magnificent
hair!"

The door opened. Everybody gasped.

A tidal wave of hair poured out of the door and into the hall. In the middle stood Amanda. She seemed to be floating on a sea of ringlets and curls.

"Your hair," said her family and friends, "your hair, it's, it's, it's . . ."

"It's perfect," said Amanda. And indeed, Amanda looked like an angel, with a halo of short, curly hair.

"You're right," said her father. And before they were done cleaning up, everyone agreed Amanda looked perfect in short hair.

And anyhow, thought Amanda, I can always grow it back.